MAKING THE GRADE

EASY POPULAR PIECES FOR YOUNG FLAUTISTS. SELECTED AND ARRANGED BY JERRY LANNING

Exclusive Distributors:
Music Sales Limited
Newmarket Road, Bury St. Edmunds, Suffolk IP33 3YB.
This book © copyright 1992 Chester Music.
ISBN 0-7119-2916-5
Order No. CH59998
Cover designed by Pemberton and Whitefoord
Typeset by Pemberton and Whitefoord
Printed in the United Kingdom by
Caligraving Limited, Thetford, Norfolk.

Chester Music

(A division of Music Sales Limited)
8/9 Frith Street, London W1V 5TZ.

INTRODUCTION

This collection of 16 popular tunes has been carefully arranged and graded to provide attractive teaching repertoire for young flautists. The familiarity of the material will stimulate pupils' enthusiasm and encourage their practice.

The technical demands of the solo part increase progressively up to the standard of Associated Board Grade 2. The piano accompaniments are simple yet effective and should be within the range of most pianists.

Breath marks are given throughout, showing the most musically desirable places to take a breath. Students may also need to take additional breaths when learning a piece or practising at a slower tempo, and suitable opportunities are indicated by breath marks in brackets.

GREENSLEEVES

Traditional.

This tune dates from Elizabethan times.
Notice that the Cs are sometimes sharp and sometimes natural.

ANNIE'S SONG

Words & Music by John Denver.

'Annie's Song' was made popular as a flute solo by James Galway.
Play it as smoothly as possible, and make sure you hold all the notes for their full value.

Flowing

IMAGINE

Words & Music by John Lennon.

Notice the way the opening two-bar phrase is repeated, with slight variations.

If you have problems with bar 15, practise it slowly, counting in quavers.

Moderately slow

SAILING

Words & Music by Gavin Sutherland.

This was a big hit for Rod Stewart. You will need good breath control,
and you should try to avoid using the bracketed breath marks as far as possible.

Slow beat

MULL OF KINTYRE

Words & Music by McCartney & Laine

Look out for the quaver/dotted crotchet group in bar 4 and elsewhere,
and make sure the rhythm is really accurate. Don't be late playing the second note in bar 14.

SKYE BOAT SONG

Traditional.

This is one of the best known Scottish melodies. It needs a sustained sound and smooth playing.

NELLIE THE ELEPHANT

Words by Ralph Butler. Music by Peter Hart.

Watch out for the key change.
This piece starts in D minor, but the chorus is in D major (F sharps and C sharps).

TULIPS FROM AMSTERDAM

English Words by Gene Martyn. Original Words by Neumann & Bader. Music by Ralf Arnie.

Here's a cheerful tune. It's not very difficult, but needs to swing along at a good pace.
Notice the g sharps towards the end.

Bright waltz

GREENSLEEVES

Traditional.

This tune dates from Elizabethan times.

Notice that the Cs are sometimes sharp and sometimes natural.

ANNIE'S SONG

Words & Music by John Denver.

'Annie's Song' was made popular as a flute solo by James Galway.

Play it as smoothly as possible, and make sure you hold all the notes for their full value.

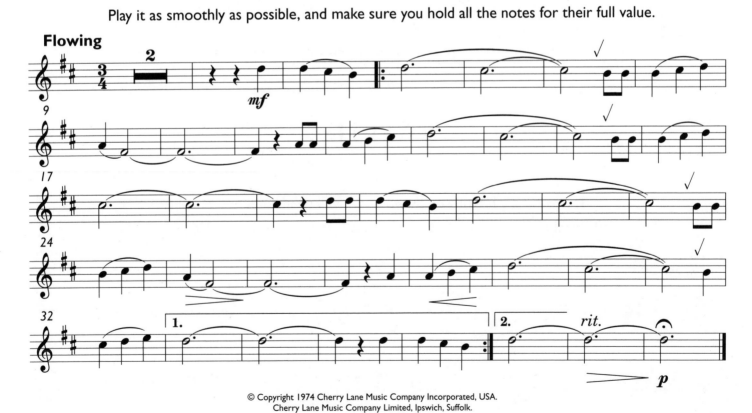

IMAGINE

Words & Music by John Lennon

Notice the way the opening two-bar phrase is repeated, with slight variations.

If you have problems with bar 15, practise it slowly, counting in quavers.

SAILING

Words & Music by Gavin Sutherland.

This was a big hit for Rod Stewart. You will need good breath control,

and you should try to avoid using the bracketed breath marks as far as possible.

MULL OF KINTYRE

Words & Music by McCartney & Laine.

Look out for the quaver/dotted crotchet group in bar 4 and elsewhere,

and make sure the rhythm is really accurate. Don't be late playing the second note in bar 14.

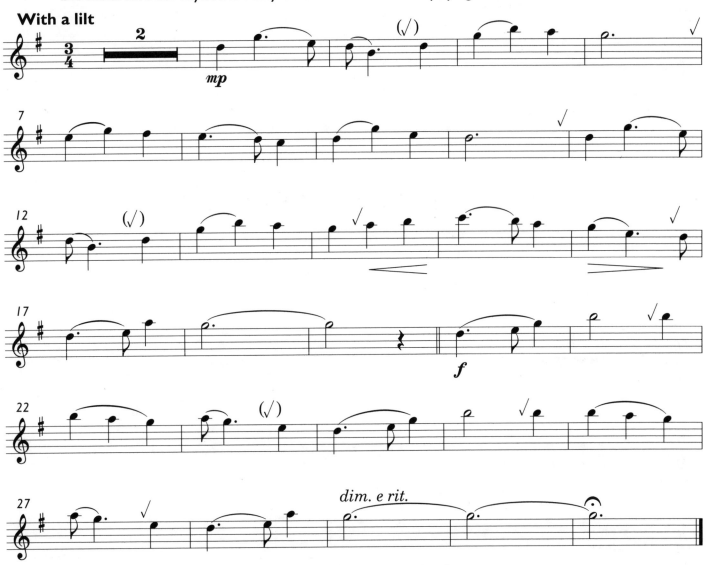

3

SKYE BOAT SONG

Traditional.

This is one of the best known Scottish melodies. It needs a sustained sound and smooth playing.

Gently moving

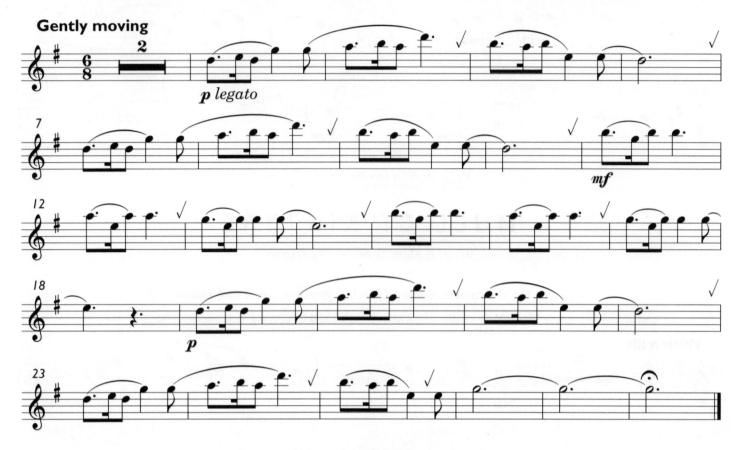

NELLIE THE ELEPHANT

Words by Ralph Butler. Music by Peter Hart.

Watch out for the key change.
This piece starts in D minor, but the chorus is in D major (F sharps and C sharps).

Moderately

TULIPS FROM AMSTERDAM

English Words by Gene Martyn. Original Words by Neumann & Bader. Music by Ralf Arnie.

Here's a cheerful tune. It's not very difficult, but needs to swing along at a good pace.

Notice the g sharps towards the end.

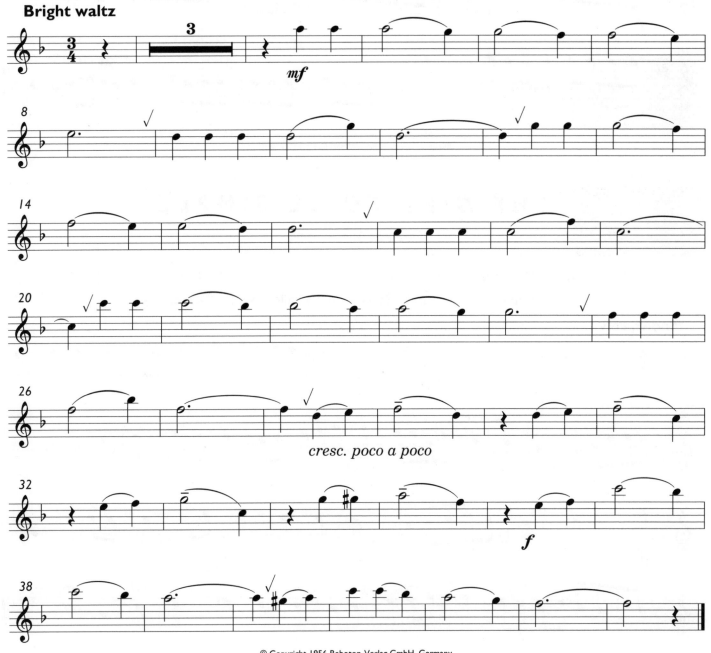

AUTUMN (FROM 'THE FOUR SEASONS')

By Antonio Vivaldi.

This theme comes from one of the most popular works in the classical repertoire.

The opening phrase is repeated *piano*, an octave lower.

THE GIFT TO BE SIMPLE

Traditional Shaker Hymn.

Also known as 'The Lord Of The Dance', this very well known hymn tune was used by the American composer Aaron Copland in his ballet 'Appalachian Spring'.

BRIGHT EYES

Words & Music by Mike Batt.

This is the theme from the film 'Watership Down'. Be careful to play the rhythms accurately, particularly the syncopated quaver/crotchet/quaver groups. Count bar 18 carefully.

WHO DO YOU THINK YOU ARE KIDDING MR HITLER?

Words by Jimmy Perry. Music by Jimmy Perry and Derek Taverner.

You will recognise this as the theme from the very popular TV series 'Dad's Army'.
Look out for the accidentals, and pay special attention to the final phrase.

YELLOW SUBMARINE

Words & Music by John Lennon & Paul McCartney.

This Beatles number needs to be played with a tight, accurate rhythm — don't slip into triplets in the chorus.
Notice that the chorus is repeated an octave higher.

VINCENT

Words & Music by Don McLean.

Keep a steady tempo, and let the quaver passages flow smoothly.

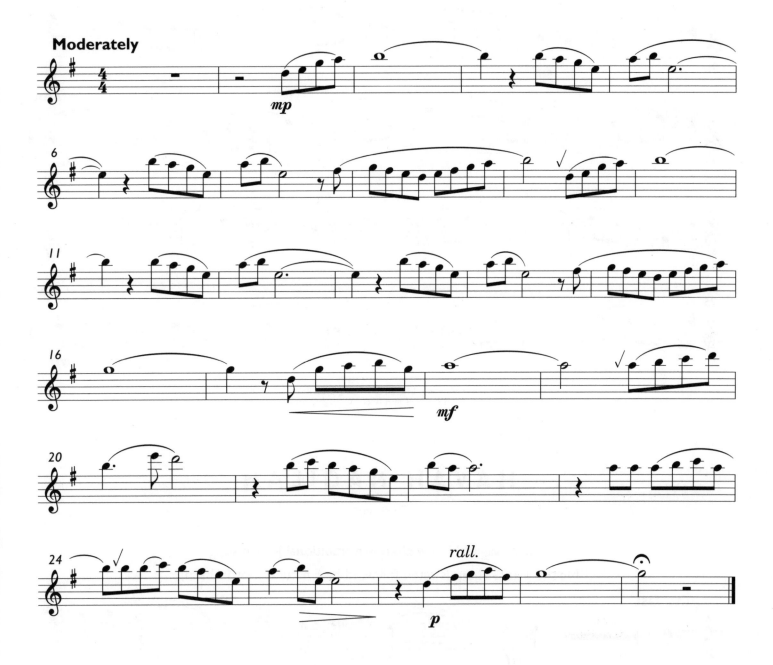

LAST OF THE SUMMER WINE

Composed by Ronnie Hazlehurst.

This is the theme from the long-running TV series.
Look out for the E flats in bars 25 to 27 as the music modulates through C minor.

HAVAH NAGILAH

Traditional.

'Havah Nagilah' is a well-known traditional Jewish song.
Notice that G sharp is often followed by F natural (not F sharp).

4/03 (47263)

CHESTER MUSIC
(A division of Music Sales Limited)
8/9 Frith Street, London W1V 5TZ

Order No: CH59998

AUTUMN
FROM 'THE FOUR SEASONS'

By Antonio Vivaldi.

This theme comes from one of the most popular works in the classical repertoire.

The opening phrase is repeated *piano*, an octave lower.

Allegro

THE GIFT TO BE SIMPLE

Traditional Shaker Hymn.

Also known as 'The Lord Of The Dance', this very well known hymn tune was used by the American composer Aaron Copland in his ballet 'Appalachian Spring'.

Moderately

BRIGHT EYES

Words & Music by Mike Batt.

This is the theme from the film 'Watership Down'. Be careful to play the rhythms accurately, particularly the syncopated quaver/crotchet/quaver groups. Count bar 18 carefully.

Moderately

WHO DO YOU THINK YOU ARE KIDDING MR HITLER?

Words by Jimmy Perry. Music by Jimmy Perry and Derek Taverner.

You will recognise this as the theme from the very popular TV series 'Dad's Army'.
Look out for the accidentals, and pay special attention to the final phrase.

March tempo

23

YELLOW SUBMARINE

Words & Music by John Lennon & Paul McCartney.

This Beatles number needs to be played with a tight, accurate rhythm — don't slip into triplets in the chorus.
Notice that the chorus is repeated an octave higher.

Like a march

VINCENT

Words & Music by Don McLean.

Keep a steady tempo, and let the quaver passages flow smoothly.

Moderately

LAST OF THE SUMMER WINE

Composed by Ronnie Hazlehurst.

This is the theme from the long-running TV series.
Look out for the E flats in bars 25 to 27 as the music modulates through C minor.

HAVAH NAGILAH

Traditional.

'Havah Nagilah' is a well-known traditional Jewish song.

Notice that G sharp is often followed by F natural (not F sharp).

4/03 (47263)